P9-DXN-979

Donated by
SAN RAMON LIBRARY FOUNDATION
100 Montgomery • San Ramon • California 94583

THE WRONG SIDE OF THE BED

WITHDRAWN

Lisa M. Bakos

illustrated by Anna Raff

G. P. PUTNAM'S SONS

For Steve, Alec, Jillian, and Josef—
the bright side of all my days
—L.M.B.

For Joel, who makes every day better
—A.R.

G. P. PUTNAM'S SONS
an imprint of Penguin Random House LLC
375 Hudson Street
New York, NY 10014

Text copyright © 2016 by Lisa M. Bakos. Illustrations copyright © 2016 by Anna Raff.
Penguin supports copyright. Copyright fuels creativity, encourages diverse voices, promotes free speech,
and creates a vibrant culture. Thank you for buying an authorized edition of this book and for complying with
copyright laws by not reproducing, scanning, or distributing any part of it in any form without permission.
You are supporting writers and allowing Penguin to continue to publish books for every reader.

G. P. Putnam's Sons is a registered trademark of Penguin Random House LLC.

Library of Congress Cataloging-in-Publication Data
Bakos, Lisa M.
Wrong side of the bed / Lisa M. Bakos ; illustrated by Anna Raff.   pages cm
Summary: "A whimsical assortment of havoc-wreaking animals help inspire
a young girl to turn her rotten day around"—Provided by publisher.
[1. Day—Fiction. 2. Animals—Fiction. 3. Humorous stories.] I. Raff, Anna, illustrator. II. Title.
PZ7.1.B355Wr 2016   [E]—dc23   2015009069
Manufactured in China by RR Donnelley Asia Printing Solutions Ltd.
ISBN 978-0-399-16572-6
1 3 5 7 9 10 8 6 4 2

Design by Annie Ericsson. Text set in Mikado.
The illustrations were made with sumi ink washes that were assembled and colored digitally.

One morning, Lucy woke up
on the wrong side of the bed.

Her hair was tangled, her pajamas were rumpled,

and she could only find *one* bunny slipper.

Apparently, it was going to be a

one **bunny slipper** sort of day.

Lucy was supposed to make her bed,
but a porcupine was causing a *very* prickly lump.

She poked him, but he refused to budge.

Instead, he wanted to *snuggle*.

Surely, it was a **very prickly**,
one **bunny slipper** sort of day.

Lucy could not find matching socks,
so she wore one with stripes and one with dots.

The octopus in her drawers did *not* seem
to have a problem finding matching socks.

Or ones without holes.

Clearly, it was a
mismatched socks, *very* **prickly**,
one **bunny slipper** sort of day.

Lucy poured too much syrup on her pancakes
and got a sticky stain on her new dress.

A big brown bear tried to lick it off.

He only smeared it *in*.

Evidently, it was a **sticky stain**,
mismatched socks, *very* **prickly**,
one **bunny slipper** sort of day.

Lucy missed the bus and had to ride her bike to school.

The elephant on her handlebars missed the bus, too.

He also missed it *after* school.

Certainly, it was a

miss the bus,
    sticky stain,
        mismatched socks,
            very **prickly**,
                one **bunny slipper** sort of day.

Lucy was late for ballet,
and *all* the tutus were taken.

To make matters worse,
a hippo leapt by wearing three.

The hippo wore them well.

Obviously, it was a **late for ballet**,
miss the bus, **sticky stain**,
mismatched socks,
very **prickly**,
one **bunny slipper** sort of day.

Lucy was not allowed to have ice cream
with sprinkles until she ate her broccoli.

The pig dining next to her ate *his* broccoli.

He even had seconds.

Sadly, it was an **eat your broccoli**,
late for ballet, **miss the bus**, sticky stain,
mismatched socks, *very* prickly,
one bunny slipper sort of day.

Lucy had to take a bath,
but she was all out of bubbles.

The penguins next to her
decided to make their own.

They were *terribly* good at it.

Unmistakably, it was a **smelly bubbles**, **eat your broccoli**, **late for ballet**, **miss the bus**, sticky stain, mismatched socks, *very* prickly, *one* bunny slipper sort of day.

Lucy could not brush her teeth
because a crocodile had taken
her toothbrush.

He took *forever* to floss.

Unquestionably, it was a **no toothbrush**,
smelly bubbles, eat your broccoli,
late for ballet, miss the bus, sticky stain,
mismatched socks, *very* prickly,
one bunny slipper sort of day.

Lucy climbed into bed, but *someone* was hogging the covers, and *no one* could agree on the same bedtime story.

The penguins started a pillow fight.

Undoubtedly,
it had been a
feathers everywhere,
no toothbrush,
smelly bubbles,
eat your broccoli,
late for ballet,
miss the bus, sticky stain,
mismatched socks, *very* prickly,
one bunny slipper sort of day.

The next morning, Lucy woke up
on the wrong side of the bed.

Her hair was tangled, her pajamas were rumpled,
and she could only find *one* bunny slipper.

Unfortunately, it looked like it was going to be another one bunny slipper sort of day.

Until, that is, Lucy decided to put on . . .

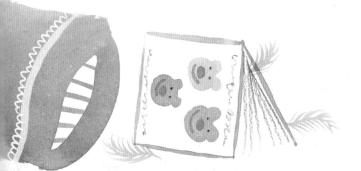

. . . galoshes.

Fortunately, it was going to be a galoshes sort of day.

CONTRA COSTA COUNTY LIBRARY

31901059974206